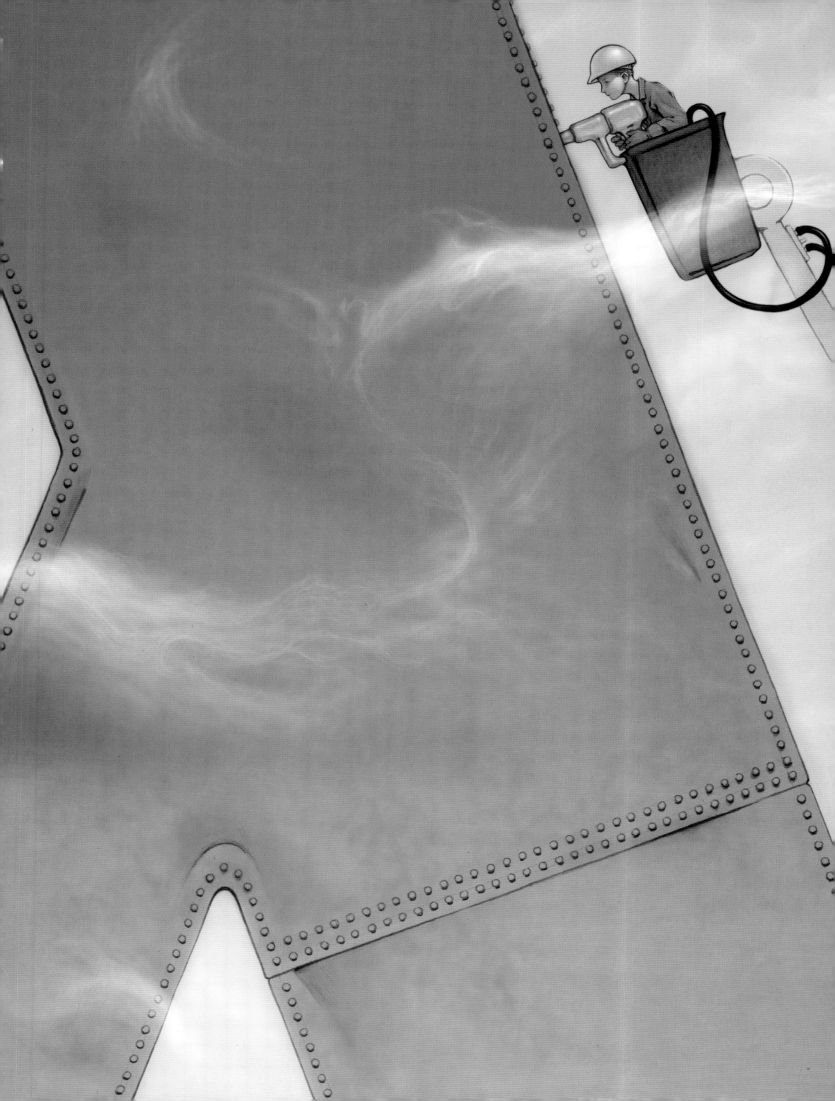

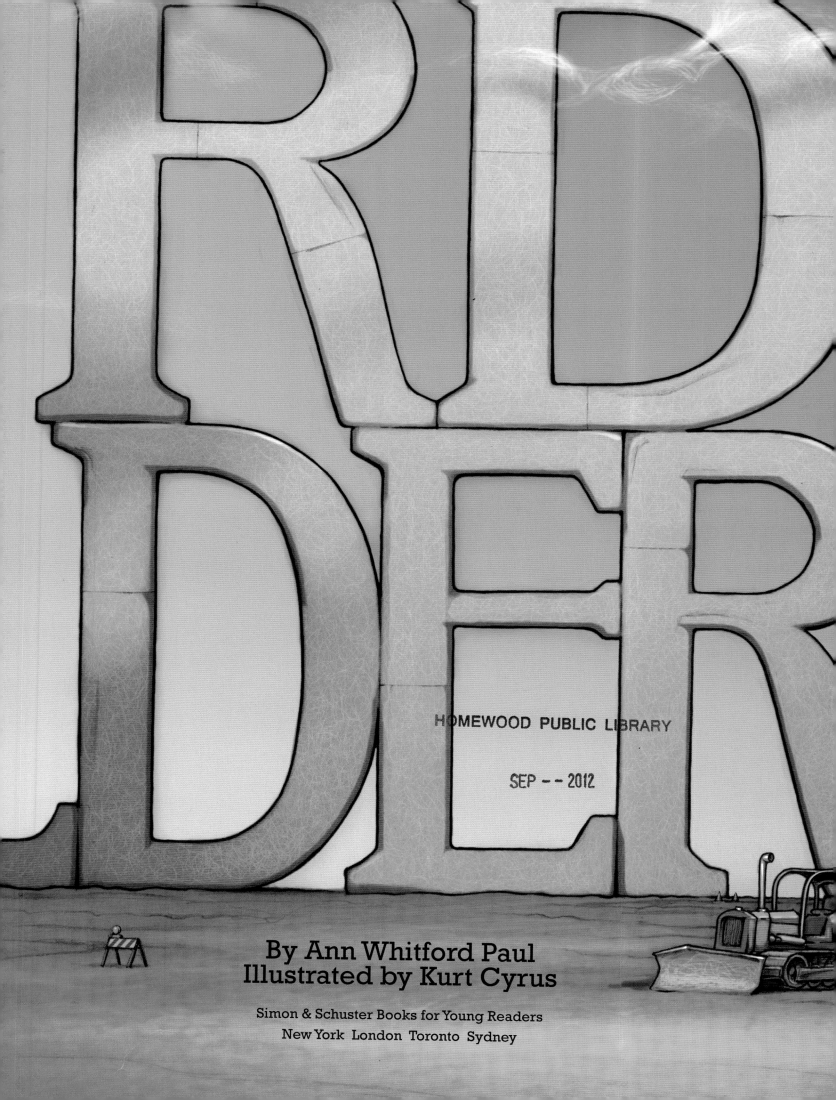

By Ann Whitford Paul
Illustrated by Kurt Cyrus

Simon & Schuster Books for Young Readers
New York London Toronto Sydney

Begin your new construction with twenty-six letters.

Hammer *a* through *z* into words.

Pile your words like blocks

into sentence towers—

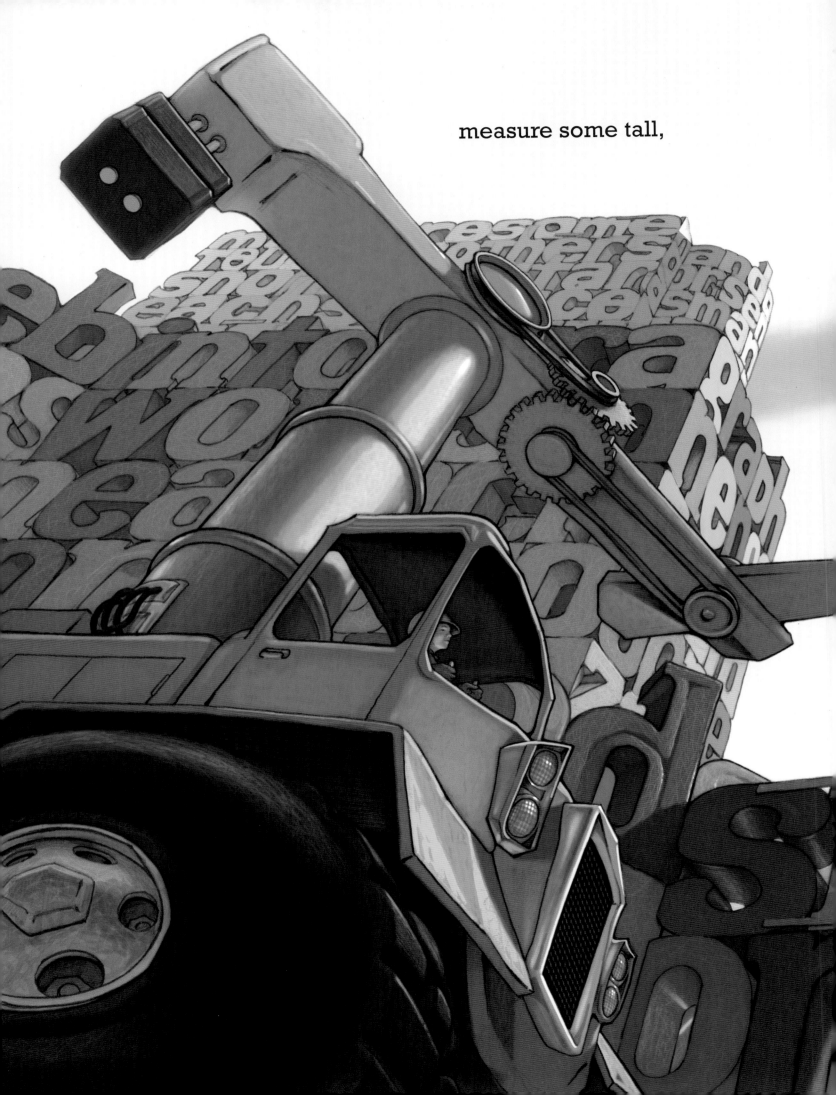

measure some tall,

saw others short.

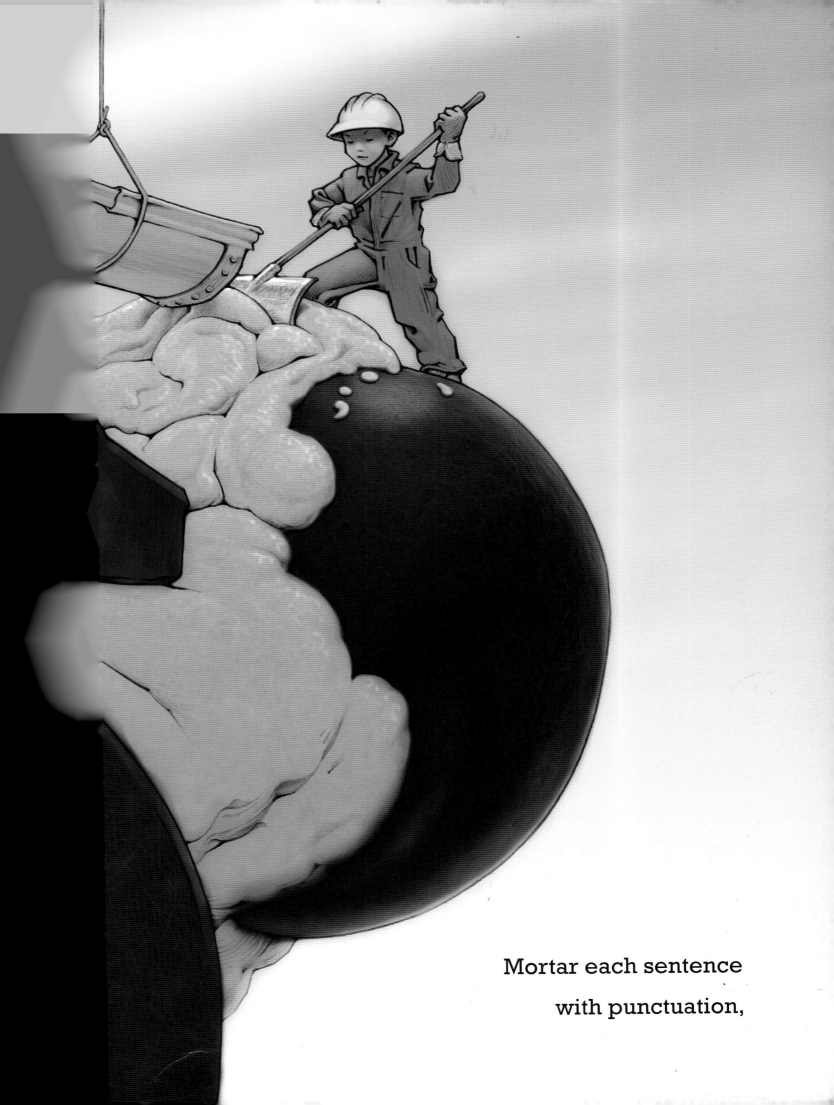

Mortar each sentence

with punctuation,

then frame your sentences

into paragraph villages,

stack your paragraphs

into chapter cities.

Keep on building

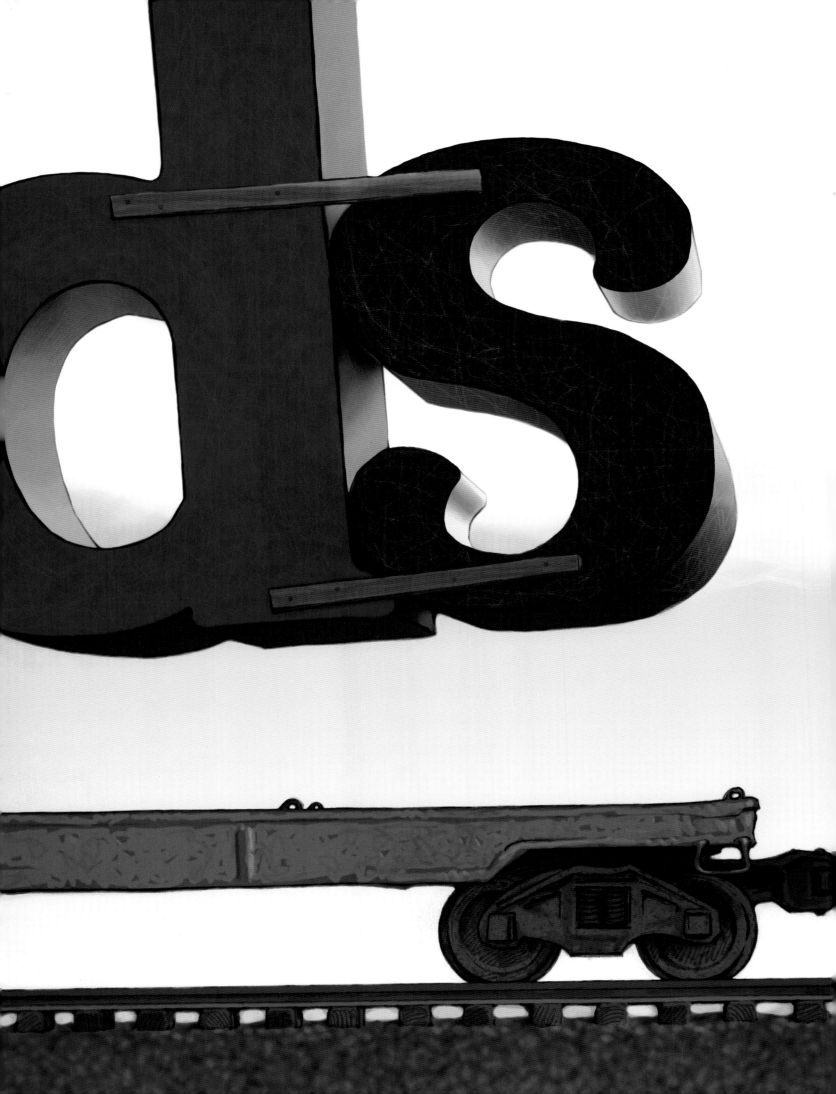

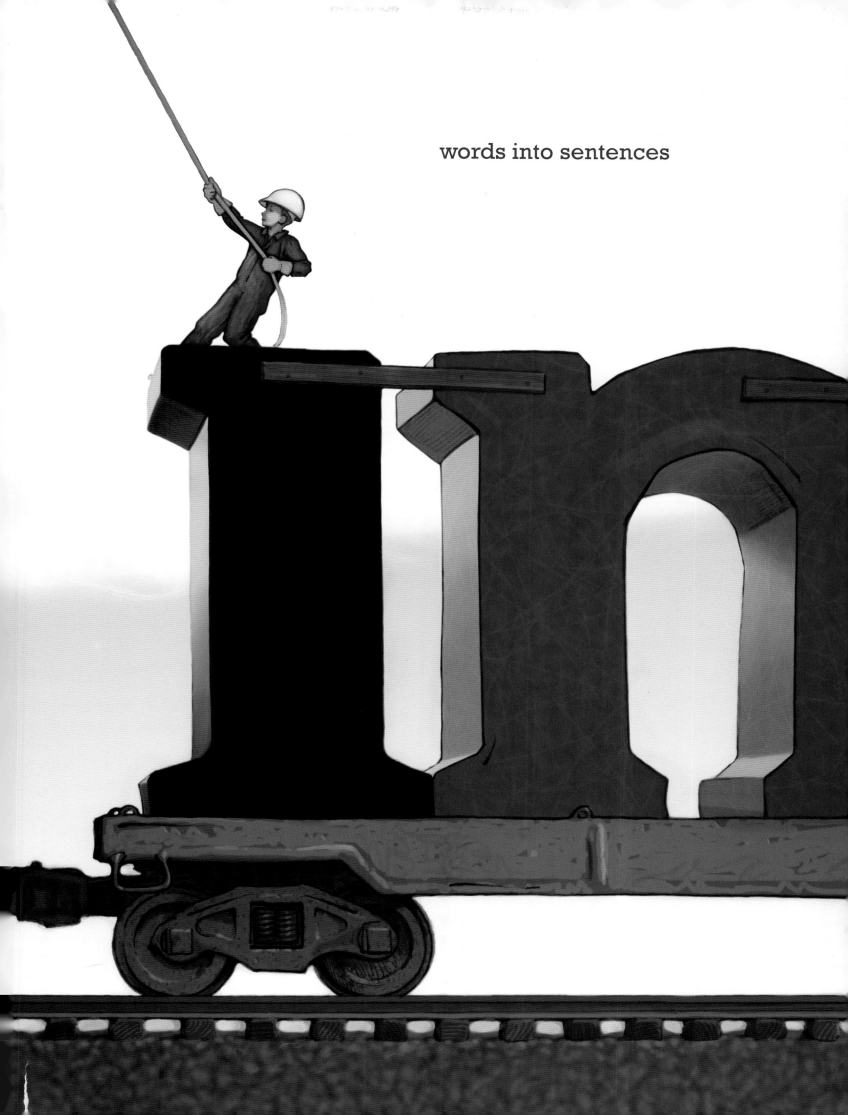

words into sentences

sentences into paragraphs,

paragraphs into chapters

a whole world of book.

For word builders everywhere, especially Lee Bennett Hopkins
—A. W. P.

SIMON & SCHUSTER BOOKS FOR YOUNG READERS
An imprint of Simon & Schuster Children's Publishing Division
1230 Avenue of the Americas, New York, New York 10020
Text copyright © 2009 by Ann Whitford Paul
Illustrations copyright © 2009 by Kurt Cyrus
SIMON & SCHUSTER BOOKS FOR YOUNG READERS is a trademark of Simon & Schuster, Inc.
Book design by Lucy Ruth Cummins
The text for this book is set in Rockwell.
The illustrations for this book are rendered in pencil, and digital color.
Manufactured in China
2 4 6 8 10 9 7 5 3 1
Library of Congress Cataloging-in-Publication Data
Paul, Ann Whitford.
Word builder / Ann Whitford Paul ; illustrated by Kurt Cyrus. — 1st ed.
p. cm.
Summary: Text explains how putting letters into words, words into sentences,
sentences into paragraphs, paragraphs into chapters, ends up creating a book.
ISBN-13: 978-1-4169-3981-8 (hardcover)
ISBN-10: 1-4169-3981-4 (hardcover)
[1. Vocabulary—Fiction.] I. Cyrus, Kurt, ill. II. Title.
PZ7.P278338Wo 2009
[E]—dc22
2007045244